About the Book

It all began the day Danny thought he saw a man following his friend Professor Bullfinch.   Lately, the Professor had been very busy working on a project he wouldn't even tell Danny Dunn about.   That's when Danny's curiosity started to work overtime.

Numerous phone calls between the Professor and Washington, the Professor's mysterious morning walks into the Midston countryside, plus the strange black car parked across the street added up to just one thing to Danny—Professor Euclid Bullfinch was working on a secret government job and enemy spies were out to get him!

To the rescue come Dan, his friends Irene Miller and Joe Pearson, and a tough little terrier named Cecil.

What happens to them, and to the Professor, when they accidentally switch on the Professor's latest invention will keep Danny Dunn fans reading on the edge of their chairs all the way to the end.

See back cover for reviews of other Danny Dunn books

DANNY DUNN
and the
Smallifying Machine

by Jay Williams and Raymond Abrashkin

illustrated by Paul Sagsoorian

McGRAW-HILL BOOK COMPANY

New York • Toronto • London • Sydney
St. Louis • San Francisco • Mexico • Panama

Also by Jay Williams and Raymond Abrashkin

DANNY DUNN AND THE ANTI-GRAVITY PAINT
DANNY DUNN AND THE AUTOMATIC HOUSE
DANNY DUNN AND THE FOSSIL CAVE
DANNY DUNN AND THE HEAT RAY
DANNY DUNN AND THE HOMEWORK MACHINE
DANNY DUNN ON A DESERT ISLAND
DANNY DUNN ON THE OCEAN FLOOR
DANNY DUNN AND THE WEATHER MACHINE
DANNY DUNN, TIME TRAVELER
DANNY DUNN AND THE VOICE FROM SPACE

ACKNOWLEDGMENTS

The authors are grateful to Dr. John Atwood, Chief of Research, Perkin Elmer Inc., and to Professor Armand Siegel, Boston University, for their invaluable advice and assistance.

Contents

ONE

The Parachute Jumper

A loud clatter of feet disturbed the morning peace of Elm Street. Around the corner came, first, a gray cat moving like a satellite off a launching pad, then a small black and white terrier on a leash, and panting at the other end of the leash a tall, thin, sad-looking boy named Joe Pearson.

The cat doubled back on its tracks and shot up into a tree. The terrier skidded to a stop. The boy fell over him. For a few minutes they were scrambled together, and then Joe sat up holding the little dog firmly in his arms.

"Let's get things straight, Cecil," he said. "You aren't taking me out for my exercise. *I'm* taking *you.*"

The dog looked at him seriously. "Urf!" he said, and began vigorously kissing Joe's nose.

"All right, all right," Joe spluttered. He lifted his chin, hugging the dog to keep him quiet. "The things I do for money," he groaned.

Suddenly, he froze. With his face upturned that way, his gaze had fallen on a neighboring rooftop where something very odd was happening. There was a flat space with a low railing, on top of the roof between two tall chimneys. A boy had come out of a trap door onto this space, with a bundle in his arms. As he straightened, his red hair gleamed in the early sunlight. He walked to the railing and looked thoughtfully down.

"It's Danny!" Joe whispered. "He's going to jump! He must have failed his exams."

He sprang to his feet. At top speed, he rushed across to the house. He flung open the back door and burst into the kitchen.

"Mrs. Dunn!" he shouted.

No one was about. He darted into the hall and up the stairs, saying, "Don't jump don't jump don't jump." Then up another flight of stairs to the attic door. "Don'tjumpdon't-jump," he gasped. Into the attic he pounded. A ladder led to the open trap door, and Joe clambered up it.

He came out on the roof just in time to see something go hurtling into space. Down it fell with a great flapping and fluttering, and landed with a thump on the lawn, where it lay still.

"Danny!" Joe squeaked, his breath gone.

"What's the trouble?" said the red-headed boy behind him.

Joe whirled. "Danny!" he cried. "You

jumped! My best friend! And now you're lying down there, smashed to bits. Why did you do it? Why—?"

He broke off short. "What are you doing up here?" he demanded. "You're supposed to be lying dead down there."

"You sound disappointed," Danny grinned.

Joe grabbed him by the arm. "Then if it wasn't you," he said, "who was it? Who did you throw off the roof?"

"Take it easy, Joe," Danny replied, calmly. "It was just an experiment."

"Aha! So you murdered somebody just for an experiment. You're worse than Franken-stein."

"You've been watching too much TV," Danny giggled. "It was a box full of stones with a para-chute tied to it. And," he added, more soberly, looking over at the object on the lawn, "it looks as if the parachute didn't work. Maybe Miss Arnold was right after all, although I hate to ad-mit it."

"Right about what?" asked Joe.

"A few days before school ended, I was having a talk with her after class and she said a parachute was more complicated to make than I thought it was. But maybe I just need to be higher up so it will have more time to open."

He ran his fingers through his flaming hair, staring over the neighboring chimneys. "Maybe if I could get up on the roof of the Midston Bank building downtown . . . ?"

Joe groaned. "Trouble! Every time you get a new idea it leads to trouble. I can just see you throwing a box of stones off the top of the bank—the parachute doesn't open— down goes the box, pow! right on somebody's head. Then the police come charging up to the roof—"

Danny nodded. "Yes, it would be better to do it at night when there's nobody in the street below."

Joe held his head. "Worse and worse! You'd have to break into the bank to get up there at night. The alarm bells go off. The police come charging up to the roof—"

"I think your record is stuck," said Danny. "All right. I'll talk to Professor Bullfinch. Maybe he can tell me what's wrong."

Danny Dunn's mother was housekeeper for

11

the famous scientist, Euclid Bullfinch. Danny had grown up in the Professor's house, and a deep affection had sprung up between the two. Professor Bullfinch had encouraged Danny's love for science, and the boy, whose father had died when he was a baby, treated the great inventor like another parent.

"Why didn't you ask the Professor before?" Joe said, lounging back against one of the chimneys and admiring the view.

Danny shrugged. "First, I wanted to work it out for myself if I could," he said. "And you know, Joe, the Professor has been very busy lately. He's been almost too wrapped up in his work to talk to anybody."

"What's he working on?"

"I don't know." Dan shook his head. "When I ask him, he just smiles and says he'll tell me one of these days. You know how he is when he's concentrating on something. He seems to forget about the rest of the world."

"Can't you get some idea from looking into his lab?" Joe said.

Although Professor Bullfinch taught at Midston University, on the edge of the town, his inventions had brought in enough money so that he could maintain his own private laboratory. It was in a wing built onto the rear of the house. Here he kept his library and his files, and conducted his own experiments.

"That's another thing," Danny said. "He isn't working at home."

"Oh? At the University, then?"

"I don't know that either. He goes off every morning, but not toward the University. Do you know what I think?"

"You're thinking how handsome I am. Right?"

"Don't be an ape. I think it's some sort of secret government job." Danny had lowered his voice to a whisper.

"You do?" Joe whispered back. "Why?"

"He's had a number of phone calls from Washington, that's why."

"Really?" Joe beckoned Danny closer. "Can I ask you something?"

"What?"

"Why are we whispering? There's nobody else on this roof."

"You never know," Danny answered with a

mysterious air. "There are bugging devices which can hear everything you say from miles away."

Joe looked around fearfully, as if he expected to see an ear hanging in mid-air.

"Anyway, that isn't all," said Danny. "There's something else."

"What do you mean?"

"Sh!" Danny put a finger to his lips. "Look. I'll show you."

He pointed. Below them, the front door of the house had slammed. Professor Bullfinch appeared on the walk. He wore no hat, and his head, bald except for a few thin strands of hair neatly combed across it, shone pinkly up at them. Although it was a warm day he had on his customary old tweed suit, its pockets bulging with papers and notebooks. He stopped for a moment to light his pipe. Then, with his hands behind his back, he walked swiftly away up the street.

Joe stirred and was just about to say something when Danny touched his arm. Across the street, a large black automobile had been parked

14

all this time. Now, a man stepped out of it. He bent to say something to another man in the driver's seat. Then he set off after the Professor. The engine started, and the car swung round in a circle and drove away in the opposite direction.

"There!" Danny exclaimed. "What about that?"

"I don't understand," said Joe. "Who were those men? What—?" His eyes widened, and he sucked in a breath. "Spies!" he said.

"That's what I think," Danny said. "This is the second time I've seen that car out there. And yesterday, I thought I saw someone follow the Professor when he left the house, but I wasn't sure."

"So if he is doing secret work, they're watching him. Maybe waiting to pounce."

"Right! Of course," said Danny, "it could be nothing but a coincidence. Maybe it's got nothing to do with secrets. I may be barking up the wrong tree. But you've got to admit it looks suspicious."

"Barking up the—!" Joe let out a long groan.

"What's the matter?"

Joe was already making for the attic door. He stopped and gave Danny a look even more mournful than usual.

"You just reminded me of something I forgot," he replied.

"About trees?"

"I wish it were only trees. I forgot Mrs. Wilfrid's dog," said Joe, disappearing down the ladder.

TWO

The Matchbook

Danny followed Joe down the stairs. They paused in the kitchen, and Dan tapped his friend on the shoulder.

"You'll need strength for the search," he said. "Cookie?"

"Maybe I'd better have one," Joe agreed. "If I don't find Cecil, old Mrs. Wilfrid will have me put on bread and water forever."

Danny prowled through the larder and emerged with two large slices of chocolate fudge cake. "Fortunately," he remarked, "Mom is out shopping. This is better than a plain cookie."

Munching happily, they went outside.

"How come you're walking Mrs. Wilfrid's dog?" Danny asked. "She's an awful grouch. Nobody can ever do anything right for her."

Joe blushed. "I needed money."

"Don't we all? You must need it worse than most."

"Well . . . " Joe cleared his throat. "You know I can't stand girls. They're a nuisance. But Irene is an old friend, and her birthday comes in a couple of days, and it happens I spent my whole allowance for this month on a copy of Louis Untermeyer's new collection of poetry, so. . . ."

His voice died away.

"Cheer up," Danny said, patting him on the back. "I understand. Irene is different. I'm lucky, I've already bought her present. I'm giving her a big magnifying glass."

"Well, I'm giving her a box full of nothing unless I can find Cecil. Now, let's see," said Joe. "Where would I go if I were a terrier?"

Danny scratched his head. "To a butcher

shop?   To the cupboard to find a poor dog a bone?   To chase a cat up a tree?"

"Stop right there," said Joe.   "Brilliant."

He trotted out to the front of the house, with Danny close behind.   He crossed the street and there, sitting hopefully under the tree up which the gray cat had gone, was Cecil.   The cat, curled in the fork of a big branch high above, was sound asleep.

When Joe appeared, the dog jumped up.   He put his front paws against the tree trunk and gave an eager yap, with his bright eyes fixed on Joe.

Joe grabbed his leash.   "If you think I'm going to shake that cat out of the tree for you," he said, "you're even crazier than most terriers. Ask Danny, he's softer-hearted than I am."

Danny, however, had already walked away. Head bent, he was examining the street at the spot where the black car had waited.   With an exclamation, he stooped and picked something up.   Dragging the unwilling Cecil, Joe went over to join him.

"Look here," Danny said.

He held out an empty book of paper matches.

On the cover was printed, *Fortuno's International Restaurant.   Washington, D.C.*

The boys stared at each other.   Into the mind of each had come the same picture: a quiet, elegant restaurant with small tables at which sinister international spies exchanged sealed envelopes, or whispered information in strange languages, while music played.

"How about that?" said Danny.   "I wonder what I ought to do?   Should I go to the police?"

"Maybe we just ought to forget the whole thing," Joe said, uneasily.   "After all, you haven't any proof of anything."

"Let's go talk it over with Irene," Dan suggested. "She sometimes has very practical ideas."

Irene Miller lived next door to Danny. Her father was an astronomer on the faculty of Midston University, and Irene wanted to be a physicist when she grew up. However, a friend of her father's had recently given her a book about insects, and she had been swept away by a wild enthusiasm for the study of entomology. All her free time, these days, seemed to be spent lying on her stomach watching insects of one kind or another.

That was how the boys found her, when they went round to the Millers' backyard.

"What's new in Bugland?" Joe asked.

Irene propped herself on her elbows. She flung her hair back out of her eyes, and said, "Hi, little dog. Who's the funny-looking boy you're leading around on that leash?"

"Very comical," said Joe. "Sic 'er, Cecil."

Danny laughed. "I can't imagine a dog named Cecil siccing anybody."

Neither could Cecil, evidently, because he

wagged his tail and began licking Irene's face. She sat up and embraced him.

"Is he yours, Joe," she said.

"Only for part of each day.   I've got a job as a dog-sitter," Joe explained.

"What were you watching?" Danny asked. And he added, with a worried look, "I see you've got a new magnifying glass."

"It's not mine.   I borrowed it from my Dad." Danny sighed with relief.

"I was making believe I was very small," Irene went on.   "And that I was sitting in a tree—one of these big grass stems—and watching the life of the tiny forest below.   You see all sorts of adventures when you just watch."

She set Cecil aside, and picked up the magnifying glass.   "You see ants searching for food or exploring.   They seem so intelligent that I sort of think of them as the natives of the place.   And then huge, harmless beasts come lumbering under the grass-trees every once in a while. They're like dinosaurs, but they're really caterpillars.   And sometimes ferocious hunters fly down.   Look, there's one now."

A large, deadly looking wasp had landed near her on a stone. Its sinister blue-black armor shone in the sun. It had a very thin waist, hardly more than a thread. It moved its body up and down on its long legs as if it were doing a war dance. Irene bent closer to look at it through the glass.

"Watch out," Danny warned. "You'll get stung."

"Oh, no," said Irene. "It won't hurt me unless I threaten it. It's a Pelopaeus, and it's only interested in one thing: spiders. And only a certain kind of spider, at that."

Danny, his scientific curiosity getting the better of him, went down on hands and knees to peer at the wasp. It seemed to be annoyed at all this attention, for with a flirt of its wings it flew off.

"It's certainly a handsome creature," Dan said. "What does it want with spiders? Does it eat them?"

"Nope. It paralyzes them with its sting," Irene explained, "and stores them away in a snug chamber made out of mud. You know— you've seen those mud nests on stones, near the

river. It lays its eggs inside, and when the
young wasp grubs hatch they have fresh meat to
eat.''

"Ugh," said Joe. "How grisly."

"It isn't!" Irene said, warmly. "Not any more
than people wanting to eat fresh meat. It's

wonderful! You just think about it. The wasp will never see those babies of hers. But she makes a house for them, and then tracks down the right kind of spider. She doesn't kill it, because if she did, when the grubs hatched, the dead spider wouldn't be any good for them to eat. She knows just how to sting it so that it can't move and hurt the young grubs. Then long after she's dead, her children are all taken care of."

"That's the most touching story I ever heard," said Joe. "I'm going to write a poem about it. I think I'll call it *M Is for the Million Spiders You Gave Me*. I ought to spend a little time spying on these things myself."

Danny snapped his fingers. "That reminds me," he said. "We've got a spying problem."

"I don't understand," said Irene. "You want to spy on somebody?"

"No. We want to stop somebody spying on somebody."

"Ouch! Confusing. Explain."

Quickly, Danny told her about Professor Bullfinch and the man who had followed him.

"Here's the matchbook," he finished. "It's obvious that these men must have come here to watch the Professor. And I'm afraid they may do something desperate, kidnap him, maybe."

"You didn't notice what license plate the car had—what state it came from?"

"No. I couldn't see it from the roof today. And the first time I noticed the car I never thought about its license."

Irene turned the matchbook over in her hand. "It isn't so obvious, you know," she said. "This doesn't prove anything. Maybe this restaurant sends its matches all over the country as an advertisement. Maybe those men are just other scientists trying to find out what the Professor is up to."

"Aha! That would still make them spies," Danny pointed out.

Joe said, "It seems to me this could be a very dangerous thing, Dan. Maybe you were right, and we ought to go to the police, or the F.B.I. or somebody."

Danny blushed. "The trouble is that it's also possible, I guess, for the whole thing to be a coin-

26

cidence. Maybe the car just happened to park out front and maybe the man wasn't following the Professor at all, but just walking in the same direction. If I tell the police, and then it all turns out to be perfectly innocent, I'll be in trouble. Everybody would say, 'Oh, what can you expect from a crazy kid?' Right?"

"If you could only find out what the Professor's actually working on," said Irene, "you'd know whether it was important enough to attract a snooper."

"I've tried to find out from him, but he won't tell me."

Irene thoughtfully scratched her nose with the edge of the magnifying glass. "There's another way of finding out," she said. "We can play wasp and spider."

"You mean we should paralyze the Professor?" Joe blurted out.

"Don't be silly. I mean we should track him down," said Irene.

THREE

Counterspies

Danny stared at her.   Then he broke into a wide grin.

"Counterspies!" he said.   "What a cool idea. And I've got another one.   We'll use Cecil."

He pointed dramatically at the terrier, who had curled up at Joe's feet and was dozing.

"No, sir!" said Joe.   "You're not going to shove Mrs. Wilfrid's dog into any desperate situation.   Suppose they are spies and they start shooting at us?   I owe it to Mrs. Wilfrid, that nice, kind lady, to see that her dog stays out of danger."

"There won't be any shooting," Danny protested. "We'll just let Cecil follow the trail and see where the Professor has gone. That's the first step. We won't do anything rash. We'll just look."

"We-e-ell," Joe said.

"Come on, Joe," said Danny. "You may be doing your country a great service. They may even put up a monument to you downtown, in front of the shopping center. It'll say, *Joe Pearson, Boy Hero.*"

"Mmf!" grunted Joe. "So long as it doesn't say, *Joe Pearson, Dead Boy Hero.* All right. But remember, at the first sign of danger—I mean, danger to Cecil—we go."

"Great!" Danny said. "You two wait here a minute. I'll be right back."

He ran across the lawn and pushed through an opening in the tall lilac hedge that separated the Bullfinch property from that of the Millers. He dashed into the house and up to the Professor's bedroom. He snatched up one of the Professor's bedroom slippers and ran back to join his friends.

"Now," he panted, "bring Cecil out to the road."

They woke up the little dog, who yawned and stretched and then with a wag of his tail announced that he was ready to join in any game. They went out to the front of the house, and Danny knelt down and patted Cecil.

"Just take a smell of this slipper," he said. "And then lead us after the Professor."

Cecil stretched his neck. He sniffed once or twice at the slipper and sneezed. Then he sat down and smiled at Danny.

"No, no," Danny said. "Up, boy! Follow!"

He thrust the slipper under Cecil's nose. The dog barked, and then started off so suddenly that Joe, who still held the leash, was almost yanked off his feet.

"Good dog!" yelled Danny. "That's the stuff. Find him!"

Straight across the road galloped Cecil. And right to the base of a tall tree, where he began leaping and barking frantically.

Irene looked up into the branches in puzzlement. "Surely the Professor isn't up there?"

"No, but a cat is," sighed Joe. "Cecil, you have a one-track mind."

"And it's the wrong track," said Danny.

He shaded his eyes with his hand and peered along the road. "You know," he said, "there aren't many places the Professor could have gone, this way. There are three more houses, and then you come to the end of town. He couldn't have gone to any of those houses; none of the people in them has anything to do with science. Once you're at the end of Elm Street, it's just country all the way to Bartonville, and that's seven miles away."

"Then if he was going there, he wouldn't have walked," Irene said.

"That's right," said Danny. "And neither would the man who followed him. Let's just take a little stroll."

They got Cecil away from his tree and began walking. They passed the last house, and the sidewalk ended. The road stretched before them, its black asphalt shimmering in the heat. On the right rose low hills, thick with maples and birches. On the left were fields of new-cut grass, sending up a juicy, rich, green perfume. Somewhere, they could hear the clatter of a hay-rake, and the coughing of a tractor.

About a half-mile from the edge of town, they passed a large farmhouse, comfortable and dignified-looking in spite of its peeling white paint. Some barns and outbuildings clustered around it. Beyond lay planted fields.

"Now, that's Mr. Erlanger's farm," Danny said. "I'm sure Professor Bullfinch didn't go there."

Cecil began straining at his leash, uttering eager whines. He snuffled at the road, pulling Joe along with him.

"Quit it, Cecil," Joe said. "We don't want any more cats."

"Maybe it isn't a cat this time," said Irene. "Let's see what he's after."

Opposite the farm, a cowpath wound toward the higher pasture land. With his nose to the ground, Cecil started along the track. The three children followed, Joe keeping a tight hold on the leash. Some five hundred yards from the road, the track made a sharp bend. As they rounded the bend, they saw, hidden in a hollow, an old red barn. Cecil stopped, gave a satisfied bark, sat down, and scratched his neck busily with a hind leg.

"Fine," Joe growled. "A barn. Just what we need to keep our cats in, eh?"

Danny tapped his arm. "Hold on a sec. Look at that."

Joe followed Danny's pointing finger. "I don't see anything special. You mean that steel thing over behind the barn? It's just carrying some electric cables. What of it?"

"What of it?" Danny groaned. "Use your head. Those are high-voltage cables. They run back toward the road. Why would anyone bring so much electric power to a barn stuck out here?"

"To run electric cows?"

Irene stuck her face close to the boys'. "Keep still. Make believe you're still talking but look over toward that big maple tree to the left of the barn."

They did as she asked. Danny's eyes widened.

"Jeepers!" he said. "It's him—the man who followed the Professor."

The fellow was leaning against the shaggy bark of the tree, staring off into space. He could hardly be noticed in the shadows under the leaves, for he wore a dark suit. As they watched, he took out a cigarette and lit it.

"I'll bet I know what it says on the cover of those matches," Danny muttered. "I don't think he's noticed us, but even if he has he won't think anything of three kids and a dog. Come on, let's go back to the road."

They retraced their steps in silence, until they came out on the hard surface again. They sat down together on the grass that lined the road.

Joe scratched Cecil between the ears. "Splendid animal! You must be part bloodhound after all."

"That's right," Danny said. "If that man's watching the barn we can be sure the Professor's inside. But if he's really a spy and we run down to warn the Professor, we might run into trouble. A spy might not hesitate to start shooting."

"In that case," said Joe, "let's go home. It's not me I'm worried about, you understand, but Cecil."

"Correct," Danny agreed. "Let's go home. There's nothing more we can do here now. But tonight, when Professor Bullfinch comes home to dinner, I'll warn him. And then we'll see whether we can't figure out a way to outwit that spy."

FOUR

"People From Another Planet!"

It was a rather silent meal that night, when Danny and his mother and Professor Bullfinch sat down to dinner. The Professor seemed preoccupied, as he had been for so many days, and drew little diagrams on the tablecloth with the handle of his fork. Mrs. Dunn was planning flower arrangements for the Women's Civics Club meeting on Sunday. And Danny was trying to decide how to broach the subject of the secret agent.

At last, when dessert had been cleared away, he leaned forward with his elbows on the table, and said, "Professor Bullfinch, I made a parachute to-day, but it didn't work."

"Ah, yes, parachutes," said the Professor. He began to polish his glasses with his napkin. "But aren't you a little young for parachute jumping?"

"You're getting butter all over your glasses, Professor," said Mrs. Dunn. Gently, she took the spectacles away from him and cleaned them.

Danny said, "I don't intend to jump, myself. It was an experiment. I just fastened the parachute to a weighted box and threw it off the roof. But it didn't open properly."

"There are a great many factors to be considered. You must have enough height for the size of the parachute, to allow it time to open. Above all, you have to calculate the right proportion of parachute surface to the weight you're going to drop. An interesting problem, very interesting." His eyes had taken on a faraway look. "Perhaps you ought to discuss it with Professor Siegel, in Boston."

"Professor," Danny said, patiently. "I'm not going to Boston."

"Heavens!" The Professor came to himself

with a start. "Do forgive me, Dan. I'm afraid I was thinking of something else. Now what were you saying about parachutes?"

Danny said, craftily, "You know, it's interesting that spies are sometimes dropped into other countries by parachute."

Professor Bullfinch blinked. "Are you thinking of becoming a spy?"

"Of course not. But I was thinking—er—what would you do if you were followed by a secret agent?"

"I? Followed? Secret agent? Great guns, Dan! This whole conversation is becoming much too complicated for me."

Mrs. Dunn had gone into the kitchen to begin the washing-up. Danny glanced at the kitchen door, and then, lowering his voice, said earnestly, "Well, you *are* being followed, Professor."

Professor Bullfinch's mild, round face was full of bewilderment. He looked around the room, and then said, "Right now?"

"This morning, when you left the house, there was a big car waiting across the road. A man got out of it and followed you."

"But that's absurd. Why would anyone follow me?"

"To find out what you're working on."

The Professor stroked his chin. At last, he said, "I find this hard to believe, Dan. Are you certain he wasn't a perfectly harmless passerby, who just happened to be going my way?"

"He was hiding behind a tree near that old barn, later in the morning."

Professor Bullfinch gave Danny a shrewd look. "And how do you know that, my boy? I gather you were there, too, eh?"

Danny blushed. "I—er—we took a walk, and just sort of found ourselves near the barn."

"I see." The Professor chuckled, and then seemed to sink into meditation. He pulled out his pipe and tobacco pouch, and Danny thought he heard something clatter to the floor. Before he could bend to look, however, the Professor said, "This is rather disturbing. If you are certain of your facts, I'll have to look into the matter. Let me think about it."

Danny drew a deep breath. "Just what *are* you working on, Professor?" he asked.

"That," said Professor Bullfinch, cramming tobacco into his pipe, "is very difficult to explain. Exceedingly difficult. I'm afraid you must be patient, my boy."

At that instant, the telephone rang.

The Professor rose and hurried out into the hall. Danny heard him say, "Hello. Yes, this is he. Washington? Very well, I'll wait."

Danny said to himself, I know it's wrong to eavesdrop. I really must not listen to other people's telephone conversations.

He sighed, and put his hands over his ears. Even so, he could still hear the Professor's voice, which was deep and resonant.

"Hello, Grimes. Yes, everything's going well. More than well—I think I can report complete success.... Thank you.... I intend to run the final check early tomorrow morning. What? Yes, yes, the utmost secrecy.... Splendid, Grimes. Until tomorrow, then. Goodbye."

He hung up. Danny took his hands away from his ears, and heard the Professor's footsteps going along the corridor to his laboratory, in the rear of the house. The door slammed.

"Oh, gosh!" The boy sighed. "The utmost secrecy! And I don't think he really believed what I told him about that spy."

He got up and moved the chairs in to their places around the dining table. As he did so, his foot struck something on the floor. He bent and picked it up. He took it over to the window, and as he examined it he frowned in perplexity.

It was a leather case, no more than an inch long. It fastened in front, and when Danny had succeeded in opening it there were revealed half a dozen keys, some so small that he could just barely make out what they were.

He whistled tunelessly, staring at his find. Then he clenched his fist around the little case, shoved his hand in his pocket, and went out through the kitchen, saying,

"I'm going over to Irene's, Mom."

Irene was in the garden, playing a game of croquet against herself in the golden evening sunlight. She gave the red ball one final knock. Then she reversed her mallet, stuck the tip of the handle into the ground, and sat down on the head, while Dan showed her his find.

"It fell out of the Professor's pocket," he said. "It's plain as day. Those keys are perfect, but they're too small to fit any human lock. You know what that means, don't you? They might fit a *non*human one."

"But where—?" Irene began.

"In that barn," Danny said, vehemently. "I'll bet you anything you like that Professor Bullfinch has made contact with people from another planet."

He shoved his hands into his pockets and began walking restlessly to and fro. Irene studied the tiny case on the palm of her hand.

"I can see it all," Danny said. "They must be some small but intelligent form of life. Maybe a kind of giant ant, even. They must have arrived in a little spaceship and somehow the Professor has met them. And that spaceship is probably in the barn right now! That's why he's being so secretive. Just imagine the excitement if the news got out."

"Do you suppose," said Irene, "that maybe he's been trying to learn their language all this time?"

"That's it! Of course. He was on the phone

tonight talking to his old friend, Dr. Grimes, who is the head of the Academy of Scientific Research, in Washington. He told Dr. Grimes that he was going to run the final check tomorrow morning. That means he must now be able to communicate with them.''

"Did you tell him about that secret agent?''

"Sure. But I don't think he paid much attention. He said he'd think about it.'' Danny smacked his fist into his palm. "We've got to do something. Whatever his 'final check' is, we can't let that spy find out about it.''

Irene delicately poked the keys with one finger. "I have a different idea,'' she said. "Maybe it's not a spaceship at all. Maybe the Professor has found some way to transfer himself from here to another planet. Then he could go there and bring back things like this. I read a science-fiction story once about a machine called a matter-transporter, which could move people through space and time that way.''

"Well, sure, that's another possibility,'' Danny agreed, rather reluctantly. He didn't want to give up the idea of a tiny spaceship hidden in the barn.

"We don't really know which it is, do we?" Irene murmured.

"No.   But there's one thing we *do* know." Danny folded his arms and looked at her with grim determination. "It's up to us. And whatever we do, it's got to be done tomorrow morning."

FIVE

Into Thin Air

The three young people and the small dog tramped along the country road. The morning was fresh and clear, not yet hot, brimming with bird songs. Joe had let Cecil off his leash, and the terrier ran madly away to investigate the delicious scents of mice or rabbits, and then came rushing as madly back again to greet the three friends with barks of excitement. They, in turn, treated him to the melodious strains of *By the Light of the Silvery Moon* sung in harmony.

They fell silent, however, when they came in

sight of the barn, hidden in the fold of the hills. Even Cecil settled down, panting, and looked up into Danny's face as if waiting for orders.

"Now," Danny said, "the Professor should be along soon. If he left at his usual time, he's not far behind us. And behind him, if we're right, will come that snooper. We've got to find a place to hide. Then we can watch for the spy, and when he's taken up his position, we can point him out to the Professor. That should be proof enough. Then we can figure out what to do about him."

"We have to hide where we can get to the Professor, but where the spy can't see us and be warned," said Irene. "That isn't going to be easy."

Danny squinted at the barn, wrinkling his freckled nose. "What about right in there?" he said.

"You're kidding!" cried Joe. "If that place is full of creepy little monsters from another planet, you're not going to get me into it."

Danny had the kind of look on his face that you have on a hot day in front of a double-scoop chocolate ice-cream soda. "That's just the point," he said. "If they are in there, I'm dying to take a look at them."

"Well, count me out. You die. I'll stay alive," said Joe.

"Don't be such a coward," Danny grinned, punching his friend lightly on the arm.

"I have a reputation to keep up," Joe replied.

"But if the Professor has been able to communicate with them, then they're used to human beings. If they haven't hurt him, why should they hurt us?"

"Maybe they're picky and choosy," Joe mumbled.

Irene said, "The whole discussion is just silly. I'll bet the barn is locked."

"There's only one way to find out." Dan took a breath and strode forward resolutely. Irene followed, and Joe dragged unwillingly behind, whistling for Cecil. The barn, which had once been used for hay, had big double doors and these were firmly padlocked. Several windows, with panes too dirty to see through clearly, were also fastened tightly in place. But in the rear, they found a sagging door closed only by a sliding bolt. Softly, his heart in his mouth, Dan pushed this bolt back. He opened the door, which gave a startling shriek. He stepped inside, and the others nervously crowded on his heels.

A dim sort of twilight came in through the windows, enough light so that once their eyes were used to it they could see well enough. The whole lower part, under the hayloft, appeared at first glance to be full of steel and glass boxes piled one on top of the other. These, it became clear, were the components of a computer of some kind: some contained transistor switches and others disks of tape; still others were strange to both Dan and Irene although they had visited several giant computers in the past. One end of the barn was taken up by a tangle of apparatus. There were curiously coiled wires, panels, and grids inset with tubes and switches, and larger pieces of unfamiliar machinery which reminded Dan of the parts of an electrical generator. The air smelled of hot oil and metal, mingled with the faint sweetness of old hay.

There were several large electric work-lights hanging from beams, but Danny vetoed turning them on lest they attract too much attention. In the pale light of the windows, he stared about.

"There's nothing that looks like a spaceship in here," Irene said.

"Maybe not," said Danny, in a disappointed tone. "Let's look around. If it's really small, it could be hidden among all this machinery."

"We'll have to hurry," said Irene. "The Professor may be here any minute."

They began to explore, moving as softly as they could. Even Cecil seemed subdued, and kept close to Joe. They looked behind the cases and the apparatus, and Dan even climbed the ladder and peeped into the empty loft. But they found no miniature spaceship, nor any trace of visitors from another planet.

Danny came, at last, to stare at the jumble of equipment at the end of the barn. It seemed to be arranged around a bare metal plate, about three feet square, set into the board floor. Two shining, upright metal bars framed it like door posts. On a panel next to it were some glass-fronted indicators, some calibrated dials, and a switch with a red handle. ON and OFF said two small plates. The switch was set to OFF.

For Danny Dunn, to see such a switch was to want to take hold of it. And once having put his hand on it, to see what would happen if he threw it.

He began to reach out. Then he thought, No, sir! I'm always acting in a headstrong manner. I'd better not touch it.

Unfortunately, Irene chose that moment to say, "It looks as though I was right, Dan. There's no spaceship here. But maybe that platform is the thing I was talking about—a way of transporting matter over light-years of space."

Danny said, "Then if it was working, maybe something would appear on it. Something from another planet—!"

He could resist no longer. He seized the red-handled switch and moved it to the ON position. Somewhere, something began humming.

The three young people automatically moved back. But nothing at all happened.

This final disappointment was too much for Dan. Turning his back sulkily on the platform, he snapped, "Well, I give up. Come on, let's find a place to hide before the Professor walks in on us."

They moved away from the machine. Then Irene turned back, saying, "Danny, you forgot to switch it off. You'd better—"

There was a sudden flapping noise. They all jumped.

Cecil had been nosing along one wall, and had disturbed a huge moth. It flew up, its wings beating against the wooden boards, and then sailed out into the room. With a shout of joy, Cecil launched himself at it. His teeth snapped empty air.

"Cecil!" yelled Joe, forgetting the need for quiet.

The moth sailed down directly between the two upright metal bars. Cecil sprang again, missed, and landed in the center of the flat metal plate.

The machine went cluck! Cecil vanished.

With Cecil's jump, Joe had shot forward,

shouting, "Come back!" Clutching at empty air, he tried to stop himself. He lost his balance and fell sprawling on the plate.

Cluck! said the machine again. Joe disappeared.

Irene and Danny had run forward to grab Joe. Hands outstretched, they collided in the opening between the bars.

At that instant, the barn door screeched open. Professor Bullfinch stepped inside. He had heard the commotion from outside and had run the last few steps. Panting, bewildered, he saw Dan and Irene tottering on the edge of the plate.

He rushed at top speed across the barn to stop them. His toe caught a projecting board, and he crashed into them. All three went headlong.

Cluck! Cluck! Cluck!

There was silence except for the soft humming of the machinery. A little dust spiraled lazily upward on the sunbeams that came in through the cracks between the boards. The barn was empty.

SIX

The Enormous Plain

There was, first, a terrible, spinning dizziness. Danny felt as if he had been caught in a whirl-pool, so that even as he spun round he was being drawn down, ever down, in a kind of slow-motion fall. The dizziness faded. He lost all sense of his limbs, as if he had been whirled to bits and was now only a *mind* floating alone in empty blackness.

I wonder if I've been killed? he thought, but even with the thought all thinking stopped. There was nothingness.

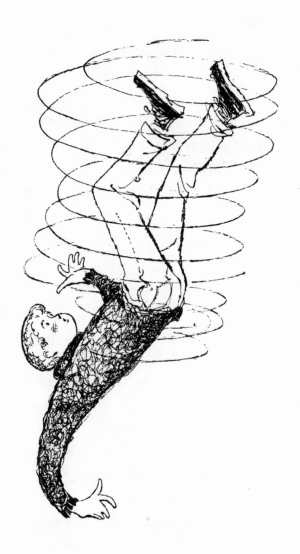

Then, all at once, with a rush, he seemed to come back together again. His body prickled all over with pins and needles. He was lying on the ground, face downward, and for a time he was almost afraid to open his eyes.

He rolled over and sat up. He was in the midst of an enormous plain, like a prairie, except that no grass grew there. The ground was bumpy and uneven, but featureless. It held a glow in its surface, and here and there faint rainbows of color shone in it. Large pebbles, or hard lumps of earth, lay scattered about. Off in the distance, a great band of brilliant yellow light stretched across a wide arc of the horizon. In the other directions, all was dark. It was not so much a darkness of night as of the murkiness before a storm. Looking up, he saw that the sky was pale gray, but tinged with the reflection of that yellow light. Still higher, however, it seemed to thicken and darken like the greater part of the horizon. He caught hints of vague shapes, up above, which he took to be the piled masses of clouds hanging in the air.

"It's either morning or evening," he said to

himself, looking toward the band of brightness.

He got shakily to his feet. The yellow light cast his shadow far behind him.

There were no trees, no bushes. No birds flew. But a few hundred yards away, in the direction of what was either the sunset or the sunrise, he saw figures moving about. They were silhouetted against the light and he could not make them out clearly. He started to walk toward them, a little frightened, but even more filled with curiosity.

Something was wrong with his legs. He seemed to be very wobbly. At his first step, he felt himself beginning to fall. But before he could throw out his arms to stop himself, he was on the ground. It had happened in the blink of an eye.

He pushed himself up on hands and knees. The biggest surprise of all was that he wasn't hurt. Although the ground seemed hard, he had landed as if on a pad of sponge rubber.

He stood up again carefully, realizing that he was going to have to learn to balance himself and to walk, as if he were a baby. "I know what it is," he muttered. "The gravity's different here."

He felt it inside himself: he was strangely light. He began to walk with small, cautious steps, his arms out to the sides. After a while, he discovered that he could move quickly enough in a kind of skating glide. The only trouble was that whenever he stumbled, or lost his balance, he fell so rapidly that he never had time to stop himself. However, he never seemed to bruise himself either, so that it all evened out.

The odd gravity affected the pebbles too, but in a different way. When he kicked one by accident, it rose slowly in the air, and hung for a fraction of a moment before dropping back to rest. He picked one up and examined it. It was jagged but light, like a piece of pumice. It had a dull gray color, and seemed to have minute fibers embedded in it, so that it was more like a clod than a pebble. He threw it away, and it bounced slowly.

The figures he had seen were closer than he had thought. The flatness of the place and the long shadows had made it hard to judge distance. He could recognize them now: Joe and Irene were standing up, and the third—that must be the Professor—was lying huddled on the ground. Cecil had been standing behind Joe's legs, but now he came bounding toward Danny, barking a welcome. It was curious to see him move. He rose much higher into the air than he had any right to go, and took longer to come down. He landed each time with an awkward flop, scrambled about, and was up again in an instant and taking another jump.

He plunged into Danny's arms and they went down together, Cecil squirming and licking the boy's face. Dan let him go, and got up again. He was used to it by now and did it without thinking. He glided over to join the others.

"Oh, I'm so glad you're all right," Irene said. "We've been scared to death."

"Where are we?" Joe asked. "I'm not really worried, but I'm wondering what we're going to do about lunch."

He made himself look so earnest that the others, in spite of their anxiety, could not help smiling.

Danny turned to the Professor. "What's wrong with him?" he said.

"There's a bruise on his forehead," Irene ex-

plained. "He must have banged his head on one of those upright bars when he tripped."

They bent over the Professor's silent form. Joe held back the eager Cecil. Professor Bullfinch's face was pale, but his breathing seemed deep and even.

"There's nothing we can do for him except

leave him alone," Danny said in a troubled voice. "As for where we are—I guess we're on that other planet, wherever *that* is.   If so, there must be people somewhere, the people Professor Bullfinch got those keys from."

"Then perhaps we ought to scout around," Irene said.   "If we could find some water, we might be able to revive the Professor."

Danny nodded.   "We can't leave him here alone, though.   Will you stay with him, Irene? You can keep Cecil with you so that he doesn't run off and get lost."

"I don't know what Mrs. Wilfrid would say if she knew I'd walked her dog to another planet," Joe groaned.

Irene looked unhappy.   "I don't know whether it's a good idea for us to separate. Hadn't we better stick together?"

"Look, Joe and I will go just a little way toward that brightness.   It's so flat here that you'll be able to keep us in sight.   Now that my eyes are used to the place, it seems to me I can see what look like tree trunks in that direction.   So maybe that's where civilization is."

"All right," said Irene. "But be careful. Don't do anything rash. Joe, you keep an eye on him and stop him. You know how Dan can sometimes act without thinking."

Joe gave a hollow laugh. "Great! As long as you're asking easy things, why don't you ask me to flap my arms and fly to the moon?"

He took Cecil's leash out of his pocket and gave it to Irene, who clipped it to the terrier's collar.

Danny showed his friends how he had learned to walk, and they practiced for a short time. Then Irene sat down beside the Professor, with Cecil held tightly in her lap, and the two boys started off.

They had not gone very far when they saw that their eyes had been deceived. The brilliant light was not on a distant horizon but no more than five hundred yards away. It was caused, Danny decided, by the sun breaking through a bank of high black cloud which darkened the whole sky. Its lower edge was an almost level line and hung low overhead. From beneath the cloud the sunlight poured, lighting up a strange jungle. They could make out the smooth trunks of trees that reminded them of immense bamboos. There were broad-leaved things somewhat like cactus plants, covered with long thin hairs. Below, rocks thrust up out of a mat of underbrush and vines. It was a pale-looking forest; even the tree trunks showed light green rather than the darker colors of the bark of earthly trees.

Danny held Joe by the sleeve. "I think I can see things moving among the trees," he said, softly.

"Maybe we'd better go back," Joe said. He broke off, and uttered a strangled, "Yeep!"

Something came marching out of the forest. It moved toward them with frightful speed, and they saw at once that they had no chance of escape.

Danny looked around desperately for a weapon of some kind. Then he fumbled his knife out of his pocket and got the big blade open. It was a laughable defense against the thing that approached.

The creature towered high above their heads.

It had a round, smooth, dark-gray body, larger than a man's, and from below they could see that its belly was armored with thick plates of a lighter gray. The body hung in a kind of cradle of legs, immensely long and jointed. At the top these legs were thicker than Dan's arm, but they tapered until, where they touched the ground, they were as thin as his fingers. They were covered with short, spiky hairs and they glistened in the sunlight as the creature moved.

It strode up to them and stopped. Far above, they could see a glittering eye as big as a soup plate. One leg probed forward and just touched Danny's chest.

He shrank back and cut at it with his knife. The blade rebounded. It seemed to do no harm to the shining, hard skin. But the creature jerked back its leg. It hesitated for a moment and then with a vast rocking movement it turned and went striding away to their left, toward the darkness. With each step it covered ten feet of ground and it was very soon out of sight among the shadows.

"Wh—what—was that?" Joe stammered.

"Y-y-your guess is as good as mine," said Danny.

They stood uncertainly, close together, neither one willing to go on, but at the same time not wanting to suggest turning back.

Then from behind them, came a familiar voice. "It was a *Liobunum rotundum,*" it said.

They swung round. Professor Bullfinch was leaning on Irene's shoulder. She held Cecil on the leash.

"Professor!" cried Danny. "Are you all right?"

"A bit shaky, but I'll live," smiled the Professor.

"That thing—what did you call it? Is it one of the natives?"

"I suppose you could call it a native," the Professor said. "Its other name is daddy longlegs."

Danny gasped. "Is that what lives here? What a monster! A giant-sized daddy longlegs!"

"No," said the Professor in a calm voice. "A normal-sized daddy longlegs. About an inch high, I should judge."

SEVEN

Trapped in Smallness

It took a long moment for the Professor's words to sink in. The three friends simply stared at him with their mouths open.

Then Irene gasped, "But—but if that's so— then you mean we've *shrunk!*"

"That's exactly what I mean," said the Professor. He took out his tobacco pouch and began to fill his pipe as serenely as if he were in his own laboratory.

"Your machine," Danny said. He found it hard to get the words out and had to stop and swallow. "It isn't for going to another planet?"

"No."

Joe stared around him. "And right now— where are we, Professor?"

"We are on the steel plate you saw in the barn. That band of bright sunlight ahead of us is a crack a couple of inches high under one of the walls of the barn."

"Suddenly, I have to sit down," said Joe. He dropped to the ground and, pulling out a not-very-clean handkerchief, began mopping his face.

Danny was examining his surroundings. Now, knowing what had happened, his view of where he was had changed completely. It was as if he had been wearing glasses that distorted things, and having taken them off everything came into focus. He saw that what he had taken for a low-lying bank of black cloud was the bottom edge of the planking that formed the wall of the barn. The jungle was the weeds and grass just outside, beyond the crack. And looking up, he could make out that the vague cloud forms in the sky above were the shapes of the machines

looming up in the barn.   He realized, too, with a start, that the pebbles lying about on the plain were specks of dust.

He pulled out the key case.   "I found this under the dining-room table," he confessed, handing it to the Professor.   "We thought you'd gotten it from another planet where the people were very small.   But they're ordinary keys, aren't they?   You smallified them in this machine."

"Yes, my boy, I did," said the Professor.   He took the keys and put them carefully in his pocket.   "They were the result of one of my tests.   Smallified!   A good word.   The opposite of magnified, eh?"

"So that's what the machine does," breathed Irene.   "And we ourselves—we must be about a quarter of an inch high."

Professor Bullfinch nodded.   "I didn't intend to reduce human beings to their essentials, so to speak.   I was going to run my final tests this morning on some guinea pigs."   He tapped his pipe stem thoughtfully against his teeth.   "Evidently, however, it works."

"How *does* it work, Professor?" Danny asked.

Professor Bullfinch puffed at his pipe for a bit. "Well," he said, at last, "it's very difficult to explain, particularly in a short time and in simple language. In effect, when something is put into the machine, the machine takes it apart and records every bit of information about it. Then it reconstructs that thing—a key case, a guinea pig, or a person—in miniature. The original is retained on file, as it were. When the process is reversed, the miniature is used as the pattern and the original is reconstructed from it."

Joe gulped once or twice. "Then I'm not really me," he said. "Is that what you mean?"

"In a sense, yes," the Professor answered. "The *you* standing here now is a tiny, but perfect copy of the you which fell into the machine."

"But I—I feel like me!"

"Of course you do," said the Professor. "You are exactly the same as the other you, only smaller."

"And the other me?"

"All the information about him—or you— and all the component molecules, are carefully stored in the banks of the machine."

"I feel weird," Joe groaned. "I don't think I can stand it. I'm in two places at the same time!"

"Yes, in a way," said the Professor.

Danny had been listening with his brow furrowed. Now, he suddenly said, "How do we get back to our own sizes and our own selves? It's going to be a problem, isn't it?"

"It is," the Professor agreed. "And I'm afraid it's a very serious one."

He tipped his head back. They followed his gaze into the cloudy dimness above where, like faint, far mountain peaks, the machinery rose.

"Somewhere up there, miles above us," said the Professor, gravely, "is the switch which will reverse the process. The machine is set for selective miniaturization, or smallifying as Danny called it. Even if we could somehow climb up there and find our way to the proper switch, all of us together couldn't possibly move it, any more than four ants could open a door at the top of the Empire State Building."

"Then we're trapped down here," said Joe.

"For the time being. However, some time this morning my friend Dr. A. J. Grimes is due to arrive from Washington. He knows where the barn is, and will get a taxi to drive him here. He expects to meet me to see the machine in operation. Perhaps we can figure out some way of attracting his attention. Meanwhile, there is little we can do but wait."

Danny hung his head. "I should have shut the Smallifier off. I meant to. But we were so rushed that I just forgot."

"Don't blame Danny, Professor," Irene put in, stoutly. "It's as much my fault as his."

"As far as that goes, it's all really *my* fault," said Joe, gloomily. "If I'd had Cecil on the leash, he wouldn't have jumped into the darn thing."

The Professor shook his head. "I have never been one to cry over spilt milk," he said. "What's done is done. None of this would have happened if I'd locked the barn door in the first place. We must all simply determine to learn from our mistakes. And I can't blame you too much for your curiosity. I've encouraged you to be curious, Dan, and so of course you wanted to know what I was working on. It would have been better if I had told you, but I've been too deep in the work."

"But we weren't here only for that, Professor," Danny said, earnestly. "There *was* a spy, honest there was. We only came into the barn so that we could point him out to you and warn you."

The Professor put a hand on Danny's shoulder. "Well, my boy," he said, "I remembered what you told me last night, and this morning when I walked here I looked behind me. But I couldn't see anyone following me. Either your spy is very clever indeed, and suspected something, or you were mistaken."

Danny could find nothing to say.

"But that's enough of that," the Professor went on. "We must all put our wits to work. Let's see if we can think of some way of getting Dr. Grimes to notice us when he arrives."

"I could think a lot better if I had something to eat and drink," Joe sighed. "I've got an awfully big empty space inside me for somebody this small."

"Not a bad idea," Professor Bullfinch said. "I think we can venture a bit of exploration. We may find some dew left in the shade of the grass, and I'm thirsty, too. But be careful, and above all, let's stay together. Remember, some of the things we meet may be very dangerous."

They set out, moving with the peculiar gliding step they had found most effective.

Danny asked, "Why is it, Professor, that we seem to have so much trouble walking? That's one reason I thought we were on another planet, one with a lower gravity."

"It's simple, if you'll just think about it," answered Professor Bullfinch. "You weigh almost nothing, now. But your muscles and bones are made for your normal size. When you are your own size, you walk by falling forward, so to speak, shifting your weight from one leg to the other and balancing yourself. Now, however, you're so light that gravity doesn't give you much help."

"But why do we fall so fast?" Irene said. "We go down so quickly that we can't even catch ourselves."

"Yes, that's quite true," said the Professor. "It's almost an axiom that the shorter a thing is, the less time it will take to move from a vertical position to a horizontal one. Think of a great forest tree when it's cut. Slowly, it topples and falls its length. Then think of a yardstick standing on one end: it would take a much shorter time to fall flat. Then think of a matchstick standing on end, and you can see that it would fall even faster."

The three young people squinched up their noses, trying to imagine the tree, the yardstick, and the matchstick.

Then Danny said, "But surely, everything falls at the same rate of speed, Professor? Gravity has the same effect on all bodies."

"Yes, quite right, Dan," replied the Professor. "But what I'm talking about is *closeness to the ground*. Since the top of your head is now so much nearer the ground, you're down almost before your nerves and muscles, which are used to a different size, can react. We'll have to learn to walk all over again."

"There are a lot of things about being this tiny that we'll have to get used to," Irene said soberly.

"Just so. There are advantages, of course. For instance, being so light in weight, we can't hurt ourselves so easily when we fall. If we were to fall from a great height, the friction of the

77

air would slow us up.   Air currents will keep us from falling too rapidly.   And since we weigh less than a feather, we won't be so likely to break any bones."

They had come, by then, to the end of the shining steel plain.   Before them stretched another kind of flatland: the wooden planks of the barn floor.   There was a distance of what looked to the little people like a hundred and fifty yards or so of rough, furrowed, dark ground.   Here and there, splinters stuck up like leafless trees.   Between the boards bottomless chasms ran straight ahead to the end of the floor.   And there the gigantic crack gaped, sixty feet above their heads. It was as if they had come to the mouth of a cave and were looking out into the sunlight of another world.

EIGHT

"The Drink of the Gods"

It was a steep and terrifying drop of several inches from the edge of the boards to the ground. However, a dandelion grew close by and one of its leaves stretched up to touch the barn floor.

"We'll use this for a bridge," said Professor Bullfinch.

They clambered onto the bending green roadway, and began to walk down. The plant swayed slightly in the breeze, making it difficult for them to keep their footing. Danny lost his balance. He fell on the smooth central vein of the leaf and went sliding to the bottom.

He stood up, bracing himself against the thick, hairy stalk of the flower. "That's the way to come down," he called.

"I'm game," said Joe. Picking up Cecil, he sat on the vein and gave himself a start. Down he went with a swoosh!

Irene was not slow to follow. But the Professor continued sedately on his way, bracing his feet against the tiny hairs which stuck up from the surface of the leaf.

They climbed to the ground, and stared with wonder into the jungle that stretched about them.

To begin with, it was tremendously high, much higher than any forest they had ever seen. The stalks of weeds, the stems of meadow flowers, soared hundreds of feet above their heads. Among these smooth, tall trunks arched blades of grass. They were like the wide overhead bridges of some city of the future leading in every direction from lower to upper levels. The ground itself was uneven and rocky, and from it rose smaller plants tangled together in some places so that they formed a roof over the earth.

The place was full of busy life. Up and down the grass roads hurried ants as big as police dogs. Ground beetles pushed their way between the stems, lumbering along like shining trucks, while smaller insects of all sizes ran, flew, or crept about on errands of their own. Nor was it silent, as it would have been had they been looking down at the scene from their normal size. There were loud squeaks, hummings, and clicks. And once, with a terrifying roar like that of a low-flying plane, a tremendous winged creature shot over their heads. It was a hornet.

"Oh, golly!" said Joe. "Is it really safe?"

"More or less," answered the Professor. "Most insects hunt their regular prey, or eat plants or the honey from flowers. Some are flesh-eaters. However we will smell strange to them, and I think—I hope—they won't trouble us."

"Speaking of eating . . ." Joe murmured.

"Yes, come on," smiled Professor Bullfinch. "I have an idea."

They tried to keep to the more open spaces among the stalks where they would not have to do so much laborious climbing. Even so, they found that they could climb with great ease and that they somehow seemed less winded, more capable of exertion, than they normally would have been.

"I suppose it's because we're lighter in weight," Danny said.

"Partly that," said the Professor, "and partly that your muscles, while still strong, have to move less mass. That's why insects seem to be so strong. You will find that you can do things you couldn't ordinarily do. You should be able to jump much higher, for instance."

Ahead of them lay a long, cylindrical object. It was fully as high as the Professor. One end showed brownish, leafy things packed closely together, but the rest of it, several yards long, was white with fine lines running around it, and seemed to be soft and thick like cloth, or birch bark.

"What can it be?" Irene asked. "It doesn't look like any sort of plant."

The Professor pushed his glasses higher up on his nose. "It is a cigarette," he said. "Perhaps it fell from someone's pocket. We can use it as a landmark so that we don't get lost."

They skirted its end and looked back toward the barn. It rose behind them like a mountain, its roof fading out of sight above, too high for them to see it clearly.

On the other side of the cigarette the Professor

stopped, and pointed with an exclamation of satisfaction.

"That's what I've been looking for," he said.

Among the grasses grew several stalks of clover. The great purple heads with their clusters of petals were so heavy that many of them bent over toward the ground. The air was thick with their sweet perfume. And a steady, throbbing hum almost deafened the four friends, as bees moved from flower to flower.

The Professor led the children forward until they were standing directly below one of the hanging heads of clover.

"Now, then," he said, "what we want to do is somehow pull that blossom down so that we can pluck the petals. Search around and see if you can find something that will do for a cord, or rope. But don't go too far away from this spot."

Hanging from the leaves of a stalk of timothy, Dan and Irene found a long, shiny black rope. Its end was just within their reach and between them they managed to pull it down. It was springy and flexible, and quite smooth.

Danny examined it, and said, "I think this

must be a piece of hair from the tail of a horse or a cow."

He coiled it up, and they rejoined the others. The Professor rubbed his hands when he saw their rope.

"The question now before the house," said he, "is how to get it up over the clover stem."

Joe eyed the distance. The end of the stem nearest the blossom was perhaps an inch above them which, by their present measurement, meant four times his height.

"I'm pretty good at high jumping," he said. "If you're right about our strength, maybe I could jump up to it. But won't the bees be angry at me for trying to get their flower away from them? I don't enjoy bee stings when I'm my own size, but one now would explode me."

"I don't think you need worry," said Professor Bullfinch. "Haven't you ever noticed how bees, flies, ants, and other insects all sip from the same flowers without fighting each other? As long as you don't threaten the bees they'll pay no attention to you."

"Don't worry, I wouldn't dream of threatening them," Joe replied. "Okay. Somebody keep an eye on Cecil."

Cecil had been sniffing at the ground in bewilderment, for all the smells were strange to him. Irene took his leash and patted him. Joe fastened the hair rope to his belt and walked back a few paces. He stood for a moment judging the height, then gave a run and leaped upward.

He expected to just reach the stem, but to his surprise he shot far above it. As he fell back more slowly, he grabbed it with both hands. He hung for an instant, and then wriggled up until he was sitting astride it, just behind the clover head.

A bee fully as big as Joe himself hung in the air a short way off. Boy and bee stared at each other. The wind from the bee's rapidly moving wings blew Joe's hair straight back. Joe gazed with awe at the thick, handsome brown and yellow fur on the insect's body, the fuzzy legs with their combs for collecting pollen, and the bulging eyes with their hundreds of shining facets in which he could see hundreds of pygmy Joes reflected. Then the bee flew off to explore another flower, and Joe gave a sigh of relief.

He tied the hair rope around the stem. "Haul away!" he commanded.

The other three seized the rope and pulled on it. Down came the clover head. Danny speedily threw a few loops of the rope around a projecting grass root and tied it fast. Joe jumped from his perch.

"I hope I never have to do that again," he said. "Now what?"

"Now," said Professor Bullfinch, "we pull some of the petals off."

"To eat? Joe said.

"For the nectar," said Irene. "Just what the bee was after."

She took hold of one of the curved purple petals and, bracing herself, tugged at it. It came loose so suddenly that she went over backward. She was up again in a twinkling and inspected her prize. The end where it fastened to the flower head was white, and inside she could see a clear, thickish sort of liquid among the fibers.

Dan was peering over her shoulder. He opened his pocket knife and handed it to her.

Irene dug into the petal and cut away part of it. With one finger, she scooped out some of the sticky stuff.

"Delicious!" she cried. "It's like—like—"

"Roast turkey?" Joe suggested. "Hot biscuits and gravy?"

"More like honey. But softer and better than any honey I ever tasted."

The others soon followed her example. They sat down on the ground, holding the ends of the petals which were almost as big as they themselves were, but light enough to handle with ease. The pocket knife went from hand to hand, and soon they were all happily eating.

"Nectar," said the Professor. "That's what the ancient Greeks called the drink of the gods."

"Lucky gods," chuckled Irene. "Lucky us!"

NINE

A Piece of Water

Joe tossed aside his clover petal and licked sticky sweetness from his lips.

"After a feast fit for the gods I hate to complain," he said, "but now I'm really thirsty."

Cecil nosed at the discarded petal. He sat up and lolled his tongue out, panting.

"He agrees with me," Joe said.

"We all agree with you, I'm sure," said the Professor. "We'll have to do a little more exploring, but we mustn't go too far. I believe we can find some water. I feel sure it will be safe for us to search for a short while. Let's be careful to watch for landmarks, though, like that cigarette."

They walked through a thicket of matted crab grass. A rusty tin can the size of an office building served as their next trail-marker. They came into a kind of glade of sturdy rough stems that rose around them like the trunks of redwood trees. It was shady here, because of the wide

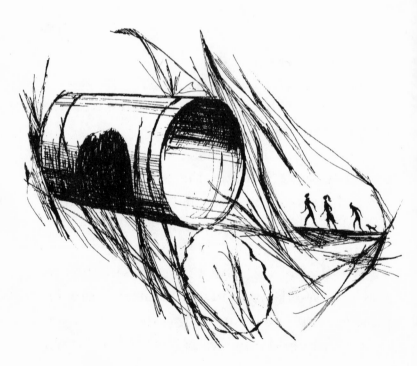

overlapping leaves a long way up. Tilting back their heads, they could see between the leaves, hundreds of feet above them, circles of white petals. It was a daisy forest.

As they stood admiring the beauty of the spot, the soft earth began to heave under their feet. Cracks appeared in it, and stones and lumps of dirt rolled away.

"Earthquake!" yelled Joe, and fell head over heels.

The others were scattered as well. Cecil was barking frantically. Out of a hole reared a pointed head. It moved blindly from side to side, and behind it came a pinky-gray body, yard after yard after yard of it. There were no limbs, no features, only wide, glistening segments. Chunks of earth and pebbles clung to its moist skin.

"Not earthquake—earth*worm*quake!" mumbled Danny, staring at the thing from behind a daisy stem. Then he called, "It won't hurt us. Just keep out of its way or it'll crush you without even knowing it."

Joe bravely dashed in close and gathered up

Cecil, who was convinced that this was the most delightful game he had ever been involved in, and tried his best to get at the worm. Irene ran over and distracted the little dog by scratching him under the chin and crooning into his ears, "Sweet old Cecil. Quiet down, now. Let the nice wormie go home."

In a short time the great creature had wriggled out of sight among the dense grasses. Danny gazed around, and said to the others, "Where's the Professor?"

They stared about in sudden alarm. But then a voice called, "It's all right. I'm over here. Come and see what I've found."

The Professor had been standing on the very spot where the worm emerged. He had gone rolling and tumbling down a slope into a kind of valley overshadowed by some wood violets whose broad dark leaves made a canopy as big as a circus tent. Underneath them, a piece of a broken cup was embedded in the earth. It was full to the brim with water and it looked like an Olympic-sized swimming pool.

"It must have rained early this morning," said

the Professor, proudly waving a hand at it. "And this has been kept from evaporating by the shade of the leaves."

They went and knelt at its edge.

"There are fish in there," Joe remarked. Then he looked surprised. "Fish? How could there be fish this small?"

"They're not fish," said Danny. "But they're not insects either. I don't think I've ever seen anything like them."

Some of the swimming things were shaped like a rather fat cigar, completely covered with what appeared to be short, transparent hairs. Others were rounded or oval, and some changed shape before their eyes. Some darted rapidly, others seemed to swim with dignity. Occasionally, one would calmly and slowly pour itself around a little particle in the water, or divide itself into two halves which would then swim off in opposite directions. They were nearly transparent, almost the color of the water itself.

"You've seen things like this before, my boy," smiled Professor Bullfinch. "Don't you remember my showing you some pond water under the microscope?"

"Protozoans," breathed Irene.

"Of course," said Danny, in annoyance. "I should have recognized them. They're one-celled animals. The cigar-shaped ones are paramecia, and the ones that change shape are amebas. But they look so different when they're nearly as big as footballs."

"Is it going to be safe to drink this stuff?" Joe asked, in a worried tone.

"Oh, yes," said the Professor. "The trouble is going to lie in getting hold of some to drink."

Danny looked puzzled. "I don't understand," he said. "Getting hold of some? Why can't we just scoop it up in our hands?"

"Try," the Professor said.

Gingerly, Danny stretched out a hand and touched the surface of the pool. It felt springy and tough, as if it were covered with a film of plastic. His hand remained dry.

"Don't press it too hard," the Professor warned. "You are strong enough to force your arm into it, but then the weight of the water

94

would be so great, compared to the size of your body, that you might be pulled in and drowned before we could get you out."

"But what's wrong with it?" Joe asked, rapping the water with his knuckles. His fist bounced back as if from rubber.

"Surface tension," replied the Professor. "You see, molecules which are close together attract one another. The molecules in a liquid are squeezed together, especially those on the surface when they're in contact with the air. If you fill a glass full to the top you can see that the surface of the water is slightly rounded. Surface tension is holding it together and keeping it from running over. If you spill a little water on a piece of waxed paper you will see round droplets form—they are held together as drops by this same force.

"Of course, when we're our proper size surface tension doesn't matter much to us. But now that we're the size of insects we'll have a bit of difficulty."

He stroked his chin with thumb and forefinger, considering. Then he said, "I know.

What we need to find is a long, heavy stick."

They searched about. Danny said, "How about this?"

He had found a large metal bar, tapering to a point at one end and thickened at the other. It was all he could do to get his hands around it, and when he had picked it up it was much taller than he was. Only his extraordinary new strength allowed him to handle it.

"It looks like—it *is*—a tiny nail of some kind," said the Professor. "Excellent! Bring it to the pool."

When Danny had lugged it over, Professor Bullfinch went on, "What I want you to do, Dan, is hit the surface of the water a glancing blow, as hard as you can. Hit at it as if you were slamming in a homer."

The nail was awkward to manage, but Dan swung with it and struck the water. A shower of silvery drops flew out. Most of them landed on the earth and vanished. But some fell on a glossy leaf nearby and remained there like clear glass marbles.

"Hurry, before they soak in or evaporate," cried the Professor.

He snatched up one of the droplets and popped it into his mouth. The others were not slow to do the same. As soon as the drops were in their mouths they collapsed into ordinary mouthfuls of water.

Cecil was inspecting a somewhat larger drop, about the size of a softball. He couldn't get it into his mouth, so he bit at it. The drop burst and soaked his face, making him sneeze.

As Cecil licked himself in surprise, Joe said, "That'll teach you to be more careful next time you eat a piece of water."

Danny, after swallowing a couple of drops, said, "Gosh, it's fun here. I wish we could stay this size for a while."

The Professor wiped his lips with his handkerchief, and took out his pipe. "I know how you feel," he said. "But we've been here long enough. Dr. Grimes may be in the barn now, and we daren't waste any more time."

Not far off was what looked like a fallen tree: a large, gray-brown object stretched along the ground. Dan climbed up a projecting branch, which had many little twigs jutting out. He stood erect on the tree trunk and peered from under his hand.

"We don't have to go back exactly the way we came," he was beginning.

There was an ear-splitting snap, as the tree trunk straightened the two immense branches which were its legs. It was a grasshopper! Away it sailed over the tops of the daisy trees, and Danny Dunn went with it.

The Butterflier

Danny felt the swift rush of air as he soared upward. He grabbed frantically at the grasshopper's back, but his hands slipped off its hard skin.
Then he was swept from his perch.

It was almost like being suspended from a
parachute. He was drifting rapidly rather than
falling, turning in the air which seemed to buoy
him up like water. He landed lightly on a wide
carpet that gave beneath him like the softest of
mattresses.

It was made up of white-petaled flowers with

yellow centers, each about as big as a sofa cushion. They were set very close together, forming a kind of gently curving floor. Near the center of the whole mass, where Danny lay, was a single, deep-purple flower. After a few minutes of gazing, Danny realized that he was lying on the head of the weed known as Queen Anne's Lace.

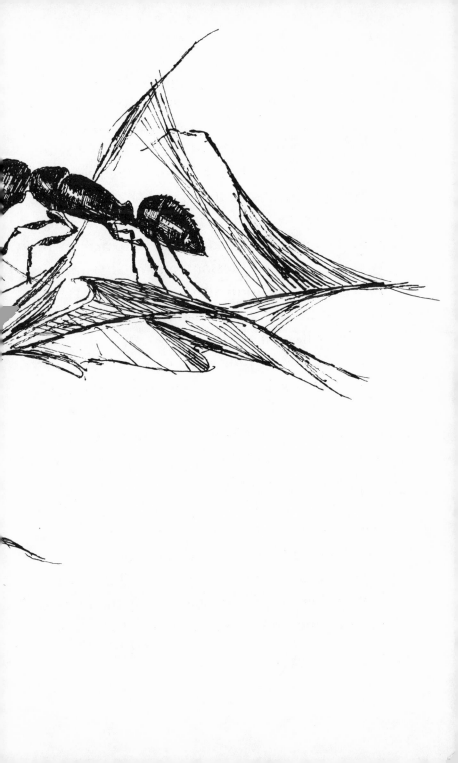

It was a busy place.   Not far off, a small, glossy-brown beetle scrambled from flower to flower. He reminded Danny of Cecil, as he thrust his nose deep in among the petals.   Now and again, gauzy-winged flies with bulging golden eyes sped down and clung with the sharp hooks at the ends of their feet while they dipped into a flower for a taste of nectar.   An ant came shoving up between a couple of blossoms and eyed Danny, its feelers twirling inquisitively.   "Shoo!" Danny said, and the ant, as if it had heard him, hurried off about its own affairs.

Danny stood up on the gently swaying platform.   On the horizon loomed the huge red side of the barn rising toward the sky.   Between it and himself stretched what seemed like a quarter of a mile of the top of the jungle: grasses, wild flowers, and weeds.

Somewhere under that forest roof, over toward the barn, were his friends.   But where? And how could he ever return to them.

He parted two of the petals at his feet and looked down.   Far, far below was the ground. Each of the flowers in the head of the Queen

Anne's Lace grew from a slender stalk. All the stalks were joined together in a thick stem which reminded Danny of Jack's beanstalk stretching down to the ground. He could climb down, although it would take a long time. Or, he reminded himself, he could simply jump, since his lightness would allow him to drop without damage. But once he was on the floor of the jungle and out of sight of the barn, there would be no telling in which direction to go.

"Oh, jeepers!" Danny groaned. "This is the worst spot I've ever been in."

He ran his fingers through his red hair, and rubbed his head briskly. But he couldn't rub any ideas into his mind.

A hint of motion caught his eye. He looked, blinked, and looked again. Up from the grass some distance away came a thin thread of blue smoke. It wavered, broke apart in the breeze, and came together again.

"A smoke signal!" he exclaimed. "Insects don't build fires. That's where the others are."

Somehow, they must have started the fire to show him how to find them. He bit his lip.

They were not so very far away and yet he wasn't any nearer to them. For if he descended into the jungle, he would no longer see the smoke signal.

A shadow fell over him. He glanced up in alarm. A butterfly had alighted nearby on the Queen Anne's Lace.

It was a tortoiseshell, its wings patterned with black, orange, and brown. It was a small and common variety, but at Dan's present size it was a wonderful sight, the gorgeous wings spreading high above him and catching the sunlight with their colors. It uncoiled a long tongue which had been rolled up like a watch spring, thrust it into a blossom, and began sipping up nectar as if through a straw.

An idea flashed into Danny's head. Without stopping to think it through, he ran forward and vaulted onto the butterfly's back. All four of the great wings were attached to the creature's thorax, or chest. Just behind the chest, the body narrowed to the waist, and then came the long sausage-shaped abdomen. Dan seated himself at the waist, which was small enough for him to get his legs around it.   He clung tightly to the fur of the chest.

Startled, the butterfly flapped its wings and soared into the air.   Dan saw the ground drop away below and closed his eyes for a moment, dizzy and frightened.   The mighty thorax beneath his hands twisted, and with each flap the wings met above his head so that air puffed about him, and he was buffeted from side to side.   But then the butterfly leveled its wings and glided slowly.   Dan recovered his courage and began to search eagerly for a sight of the smoke signal.

There it was, off to his left.   But the butterfly was turning slowly in the opposite direction. Danny examined his steed, wondering how to steer it.

The wings were outstretched.   Only once in a while did the butterfly flap them to maintain altitude. Dan knew of course that if you touched a butterfly's wings the color comes off on your fingers in a fine powder, but now he could see that that powder actually consisted of small scales, each hooked into the skin of the wing. They overlapped, like roof shingles, and were of different colors so that all together they made up the pattern. But the wings themselves were far too muscular for him to hope to control them.

Then there were the delicate antennae, or feelers, which rose above the butterfly's head like the aerials of car radios. They ended in little knobs. He leaned forward to touch one of them, thinking that perhaps if he pulled it the creature might respond. The shadow of his hand and arm fell across the butterfly's right eye. At once, the insect swung to the left.

"Aha!" Danny said to himself. "Of course! Seeing the shadow, the butterfly thinks it's an obstacle and turns away from it."

It was easy, after that discovery, to guide his mount. First, he let it go straight ahead. Then, moving his hand over its left eye, he made it veer back to the right a bit. A little more to the left, and he was almost over the patch of smoke. It had thinned away somewhat, but he could still see it hanging over the grass. He clenched his teeth and tried not to think of all the things that might go wrong. He stood up on the butterfly's back. Although he knew he would fall safely, it took all his courage to make the jump. He leaped feet first, as if off a diving board.

Down he went, like a scrap of paper, fast enough so that it took his breath away, but slowly enough so that he could see the world wheeling around him as he spun in the air. He felt his body brush something that gave way—it was a leaf. He landed among yielding blades of grass and tumbled to the ground.

He lay for a moment trying to collect his wits. Then his friends were all around him, helping him to his feet, while Cecil did his best to knock him down again.

"How did you do it?"

"Are you all right?"

"Where did you come from?"

"One at a time," Danny laughed. "I've been piloting a butterfly."

He told them of his adventures. "The smoke signal was a marvelous idea," he finished. "Without it, I'd never have been able to find you again."

"It was Irene's brain wave," said the Professor.

"When you were carried away, we were in an absolute panic. Joe and I wanted to search for you but we realized how hopeless a task that would be. Then we thought that perhaps the best thing would be to get back to the crack in the barn and wait in the hope that you might somehow make your way back to us. One of our landmarks back of course, was that cigarette—"

He motioned. Danny saw, then, the white cylinder among the grass stems. Only part of it was left. The rest had fallen into gray ash. A column of smoke still rose from it.

"Irene suggested an Indian smoke signal," the Professor went on. "And since I have plenty of matches for my pipe, I was able to light the edge of the paper. The tobacco burned slowly enough to last for a while and makes plenty of smoke."

Danny clapped his hands. "That gives me an idea," he said. "Can we tear off some of the paper that's left, and get some of the tobacco, too?"

"Why, I suppose so," said the Professor. "But what—?"

"I know," said Irene. "For a signal to Dr. Grimes. Right?"

"That's it," Danny said. "It's a way we might use to attract his attention when he comes into the barn."

They went round to the still-unburned end of the cigarette. Using Danny's knife, they cut into the paper, which was thick but soft. They were able to tear off long strips of it. The tobacco came spilling out, and they gathered up as much as they could carry. Danny sawed into a blade of grass and managed to pull several long, tough fibers loose. With these, they tied up four large packages of tobacco wrapped in paper. Then they started for the barn.

They found the dandelion down the leaf of which they had come at the start of their journey. They stood beneath one of its other leaves for a breather and looked back toward the jungle.

"What fun this was," sighed Irene. "Like being elves or brownies in a fairy tale. Why, we were like Ariel in *The Tempest:* 'Where the bee sucks there suck I, In a cowslip's bell I lie—' "

Her words were drowned by a thunderous flap, and a gust of wind that shook their leafy shelter. Something jarred the ground. Peering out fearfully, they saw a pair of scaly feet with long toes ending in cruel claws. One of those feet could quite easily have closed around all of them, and Cecil as well. A mighty beak came hammering down. It snapped up a green caterpillar only a few yards away. Once again came the thunderous flapping and the feet were gone.

"That—that was a sparrow!" stammered Joe. "If we had been out in the open—ooh! I don't want to think about it."

The Professor stuck his head out from the shadow of the leaf. "We can't stay here forever," he said. "We've got to be inside when Dr. Grimes comes, or we'll never be rescued. There don't appear to be any other birds around. We'll just have to take a chance and run for it. Quick! Up the leaf!"

They clambered onto the dandelion-leaf bridge and began to run. It was much harder going uphill than it had been sliding down, and they were burdened with packages as well. At every instant they expected to hear the clap of huge wings and have a deadly beak crash down among them. But they made it to the barn floor safely, and hurled themselves inside the opening of the crack.

They fell to the ground, their chests heaving. Joe rolled over and looked reproachfully at Irene.

"Ba—ba—brownies and elves, huh?" he

choked. "You're kidding! Give me my own size."

The place was suddenly full of a brightness that was not the sun. Dr. Grimes had come into the barn and switched on the lights.

ELEVEN

Parachuting Up

The four friends, with Cecil frolicking around them, hastened to the metal plate. It was like a dull mirror beneath them, now, in the glow of the electric lights. Looking upward, they could see the vast shape of Dr. Grimes standing near the Smallifying machine. They could not actually make out many details, for there was far too much of him. What they saw, first, were the gleaming hills of a pair of shoes, then rough, dark columns of trouser cloth like the shaggy slopes of very steep mountains, and high above those a

115

vague mass that was his jacket, with projecting cliffs that were the tips of a chin and nose.

They could not make out what he was doing, but they could guess that he was staring about, wondering where the Professor was and perhaps examining with cautious interest the various pieces of equipment and machinery.

"I am certain that he won't touch anything," said the Professor. "But we must lose no time."

Danny was heaping together the bundles of cigarette paper and tobacco. He searched through his pockets and found a box of matches. He had already struck one and was about to light the nearest bit of paper when the Professor sprang to his side and blew out the match.

"No!" exclaimed the Professor. "Great heavens! I just realized that that might mean disaster."

The children goggled at him.

"But why?" asked Irene. "Don't you want us to be rescued?"

Professor Bullfinch took off his spectacles and passed a hand over his eyes. "Just consider," he said. "Suppose you saw smoke rising from a

116

part of the floor somewhere. What would you do?"

"Throw a pail of water on it," Joe said, promptly. He caught himself, and said, "Yipes! And we'd be under it. We'd be washed away forever."

"Worse than that," the Professor continued. "There is no pail of water handy in the barn. Dr. Grimes would be likelier to stamp out a small fire."

"To stamp—" Danny shuddered. Then he said, "Wait a second. As soon as Dr. Grimes stepped forward to stamp, he'd be inside the focus of the machine, wouldn't he?"

"Just so," said the Professor. "He'd be smallified, too."

"Then we'd all be stuck here together," Irene said.

"But that still isn't the worst of it." Professor Bullfinch sighed. "The machine can only hold a certain amount of information. I believe that capacity has now been reached. If any further data goes into its banks, it will become over-loaded. Some of the data would, in effect, be lost.   So even if we could manage to reverse the process, we might not be able to reconstruct ourselves properly."

Joe gave a woeful groan.   "Let me get this straight," he said.   "You mean, it would be like losing pieces of a jigsaw puzzle.   We might not be able to put ourselves together again.   We'd be people with parts missing.   Is that it?"

The Professor nodded.   "That is exactly it. We must find some other way to reach Dr. Grimes.   Something a good deal safer—and at once!   For if he steps into the field of the machine without realizing that the thing is on—"

He didn't have to finish.   Everyone knew just what he meant.

"Let's go over to the edge of the plate, near the machine itself," Danny suggested.   "Maybe one of us could climb up.   I'm pretty good at that."

They trotted—it was a good, long city block away—to the spot where one of the pair of upright, shining bars stood.   Next to it, rising straight up from the edge of the steel plate, was a huge expanse of metal pocked with so many small openings that it looked something like the wall of a skyscraper filled with empty windows.

"On this side," the Professor said, "are the banks which scan anything to be reduced or enlarged. The process begins about a foot above this plate, so in the past when I performed my tests I put up a platform and placed the object to be—er—smallified on it. That is how I miniaturized the keys, for example. When they had reached the size I wanted, I shut off the machine, of course."

"I see," said Irene. "I wondered why the keys were so much bigger—even when they were smaller—than we are now."

Joe nodded. "And that platform the Professor mentioned explains why we don't keep on shrinking. We're all below the range of the scanner. That's why bugs like that daddy longlegs which run about down here aren't made smaller and smaller."

Danny was surveying the metal bulk of the machine. "It would be awfully hard to climb," he said in a discouraged tone. "Like climbing the front of an apartment house. And it would take hours."

"Well," Joe observed, "if you could somehow get up to the scanner and have yourself made still smaller, you could sit on one of *those* and be gracefully carried up to Dr. Grimes."

He pointed, and the others turned to see what "those" were. Rising from the barn floor, just beyond the upright bar which marked the entrance to the machine, was a steady stream of dust particles. Some were like the ones which Dan had at first mistaken for pebbles or clods of earth, others gave off metallic glints when the light glanced from them. They spouted upward like a slow-motion fountain, and new ones were continually being swept into the stream, bouncing and dancing on a current of warm air which was blowing from the exhaust underneath the machine.

They gazed at this fascinating sight for a few minutes. Then, abruptly, Danny seized Joe's hand and shook it vigorously.

"Terrific!" he shouted. "Joe, you're a genius!"

"I know," Joe said, modestly. "But how did you find out?"

"You just gave me an idea," Danny answered. "Professor Bullfinch,—why couldn't I parachute up to Dr. Grimes?"

The Professor put his little finger in his ear and shook it. "Funny," he said. "It sounded as though you said you wanted to parachute *up* to Dr. Grimes."

"That's it," Danny said, urgently. "If we could make a parachute out of something light, something that would catch that current of warm air, the air would open it out and lift it. And if we make it big enough, it would lift me along with it, wouldn't it? I'd sail up until Dr. Grimes could see me. And I could carry along a bundle of burning tobacco and paper. That would certainly catch his eye."

"Hmm." Professor Bullfinch held his chin in his hand. "I don't see why not. But—"

"It's not as if there'd be any danger," Danny broke in. "If I fell, it wouldn't be any worse than when I jumped off the butterfly's back."

"I was about to say, but what could we use for material for the parachute?"

Irene had been listening. Now, she said

eagerly, "I know just the thing. Spiderweb."

"It would be too sticky, wouldn't it?" said Danny.

"I don't mean big webs. I mean cobweb. When it's old and dusty, you know, it isn't so sticky. If you've ever felt any cobweb you know it doesn't stick to you quite the way ordinary spiderweb does."

"Yes," said the Professor, "the strands tend to become covered with dust. But if we could find some, we could peel off the outer stickiness at the spot where, for instance, Dan would have to hold on to it."

"Surely we can find some somewhere in a corner, or under the machine," Irene said. "Cobwebs are almost everywhere."

They began to search about. In the end it was Cecil who discovered what they wanted. He had been investigating the edge of the plate and suddenly let out a war cry. Under a kind of shelf of metal that projected from one section, was a mass of cobweb. As the children ran over, a small spider, about the same size as Cecil, emerged. It took one look at the excited terrier and, never having seen a barking four-legged in-

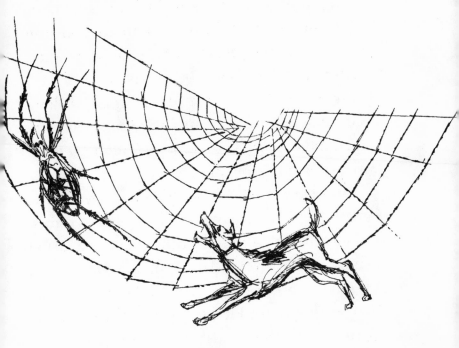

sect before, scurried off for another part of the
world.

Dan cut away the threads that held the mass in
place. Then they all dragged the spider-silk
from its shelter. They found that the dusty material had, in fact, lost much of its stickiness: it
was like handling rather lumpy nylon rope.
They managed to open it out until they had a
piece which was, the Professor judged, amply
large enough to support Danny's weight.

They found some individual threads, light and strong, and tied them to points all along the edge of the big piece. The ends were then knotted together with other similar threads. Tying some pieces together to make a long cord, they fastened on the bundles of cigarette paper and tobacco so that they would hang some way below the parachute.

They hauled the whole thing out beyond the end of the plate, nearly to the spot where the dust was rising. Professor Bullfinch instructed Danny in what to tell Dr. Grimes. Dan took a firm grip on the lower knots. He was so pale that even his freckles seemed faded. But he gritted his teeth with determination.

"Light the cigarette paper, Joe," he said. "And then move back. If you get too close to the warm air you might find yourself blown all over the place."

"It's a long way up," Joe said nervously, striking a match. "Have a good trip."

They waited, as Dan, dragging his parachute, approached the rising dust motes. They saw the corners of the silk stir as the warm air tugged at them.

"Oh, dear, I wonder if this is the right thing to do?" the Professor was beginning.

It was too late for doubts or questions. The cobweb parachute was lifting. Slowly at first, then more swiftly, it was caught by the current and borne upward.

TWELVE

The Secret Agent

Danny watched the metal sides of the machine slide past him.   Particles of dust swirled about him and occasionally tapped gently against his parachute.   Up he went, steadily and slowly. Below him, the trailing bundles gave off their fluttering coils of smoke.

Craning his neck, he saw that Dr. Grimes was standing close by.   He knew that his voice was much too tiny to carry to the giant, but he bawled, "Help, help!" as loudly as he could.

He was, by then, about level with the second

button of Dr. Grimes's jacket. Because of the spiderweb above him, he could not see whether the scientist's face was turned toward him. But all at once, he felt the upward movement fading. The warm air current was thinning out. A moment more and he began to sink toward the floor.

Then he had landed—but nowhere near the ground. He was lying on a yielding, irregular surface covered with ridges and fine, close-set lines. Out of the surface rose five immense curved columns of the same material.

Dr. Grimes had caught him on the palm of one hand.

Dan let go of his parachute which slipped over the edge of the hand and floated away. He stood up, waving feverishly. A face bent down toward him, far too big for him to see it all at once. An eye examined him. The pupil alone was twice his height, shiny as a mirror, shot through with all sorts of colors.

"Take me to your ear!" yelled Danny. To be on the safe side, he pointed to his own ear.

The eye blinked, a thicket of spiky eyelashes

coming down over it. Then, carefully, the hand was brought up to one side of the head.   It tipped slightly.   Stumbling and sliding, Danny made his way down to the ear.

He stepped up into it.   There was a sloping shelf just outside the ear-hole itself, with a few hairs growing in it like mountain grass.   Danny took a tight grip on one of them and gazed into the cavern before him.

"Can you hear me now?" he called, as loudly as he could.

A rumbling voice which seemed to come from all around him, replied, "Y-e-e-e-s."

"We're trapped in the Smallifier. Professor Bullfinch is there, too. He says that first you're to shut it off. Pull the red-handled lever down."

His perch swayed dizzily as Dr. Grimes obeyed. Danny clutched at the hair to keep from being pitched off, or falling right into the ear-hole.

"What now?" said the growling voice.

Dan passed on Professor Bullfinch's instructions for reversing the operation of the machine. He explained how a platform must be placed on top of the steel plate, and how the controls should be set. Professor Bullfinch would be enlarged first, and he would then be able to take over the operation.

"But first, put me back on the ground with them," Danny concluded. By this time he was hoarse from so much shouting. However, Dr. Grimes evidently still heard him for the hand returned to the ear. Clinging to a fold of skin near the thumb, the boy was swooped down at sickening speed. He rolled off among his friends and lay gurgling.

"All right?" cried Joe.

"Like—like—a roller coaster," said Danny. "Get ready, Professor. Dr. Grimes is all set."

The light was cut off as Dr. Grimes put the platform in place. The hand came down like an elevator and lifted Professor Bullfinch to it. The children waited, holding Cecil still, while noises sounded and shadows moved high above them.

One by one they took their turn. Danny went last. Again, came the violent dizziness, the sense of being pulled apart and scattered, and then with a rush the feeling of being drawn together again. He opened his eyes and found himself in the barn.

At first, it seemed to him that he was enormously tall. He felt heavy. When he moved, it was slowly and awkwardly, as if his arms and legs were too big. Cecil put his front paws against Dan's leg with a bark of welcome, and

Danny stooped to pat the little dog.   He felt as if he were bending down forever, and his first pat missed Cecil altogether and landed on the floor.

Dr. Grimes and Professor Bullfinch were in the middle of an argument.   This was not at all unusual: they were old, close friends and they spent most of their time together arguing.

Dr. Grimes, a dry, bony man with a sour expression, was saying, "I always knew you were impractical, Bullfinch.   And this is the proof of it.   To be caught in your own machine—!"

"Accidents can happen to anyone," the Professor protested mildly.

"Accidents are invited by anyone who keeps these three around," snapped Dr. Grimes, jerking his head at the children.   "A dog, too! What can you expect?"

Cecil pricked up his ears and smiled at the word "dog."

"Bite the nice man," said Joe, under his breath.

The Professor said, "Well, at any rate we know that the miniaturizer works."

As he said these words, the barn door uttered

its rusty shriek. Everyone turned. A figure
stood in the doorway: that of the sinister man
who had been following the Professor.

"It's the spy!" Irene cried.

The man reached into his pocket.

"He's got a gun," yelped Joe.

Danny put down his head and charged. He
hit the man smack in the middle. The breath

went out of the fellow with a whoof! He fell to the floor with Danny on top of him.

For a moment or two they struggled—or rather, Danny struggled to get hold of the man's hand, while the man tried to get his breath back. The others stood frozen in astonishment.

The spy was stronger than the boy. He got one arm around Dan and succeeded in holding him fast. His hand came out of the pocket.

Instead of a gun, it held a leather wallet. He flipped the wallet open. They all came closer to stare at it.

There was a card inside. Joe read it aloud.

"United States Government, Agent No. 4076, William Tucker, Federal Security Corps."

The man let Danny go. The boy got wheezing to his feet, and then helped the government agent up.

"Gee, I'm really sorry," Danny said, blushing, and trying to dust bits of straw from the man's coat. "We thought you were a spy. We saw you follow the Professor and we thought you were going to kidnap him or steal his invention."

"Why, that's absurd!" exclaimed Dr. Grimes.

"I saw to it that this man was sent here myself. When it became clear that you were actually succeeding, Bullfinch, I decided that it might be wise to have you guarded. After all, this is an experiment of national importance. One can hardly begin to list all the possibilities of miniaturizing things, not to mention human beings!"

"Then you should have told me you were sending him," said the Professor drily. "As it is, I think the young people did the right thing. Perhaps they were a bit hasty—"

"You're right, sir," said the government agent. "On both counts. I mean, I don't blame them for suspecting me, and they *did* act a little —er—suddenly. But there's no harm done. I saw them yesterday, but I didn't think three kids were anything to worry about." He grinned, widely. "I was wrong, wasn't I?"

"We should have known he wasn't a spy," Irene murmured to Danny. "He's very good-looking, isn't he?"

"Well, at least that's settled," said the Professor. "But Grimes, I really think you owe these young people a word of thanks. After all, even though they didn't quite intend it that way, they have demonstrated how well the miniaturizer works."

"Hmph! You always were a sentimentalist, Bullfinch," growled Dr. Grimes. "You might all have been killed, thanks to their demonstration."

"That is one of the risks a scientist always takes," said the Professor. "As far as I'm concerned, I'm rather pleased to have had the chance to experience smallness for myself."

Slowly, Dr. Grimes's face relaxed until a small, sour smile appeared on his lips. "Very well," he said. "I will see that they are mentioned in my final report to the Committee. And we shall officially call the device a Smallifying Machine in their honor."

For Dr. Grimes, this was the equivalent of loud applause, brass bands playing, and the award of a Congressional Medal.

"Good," said Professor Bullfinch. "Now, if you like, I'll go over my notes with you and explain the operation of the device more fully. And perhaps you'll want some further demonstrations of its powers."

"May we stay and watch?" Danny asked.

"There isn't going to be anything much to see, my boy," said the Professor. And with a sly grin, he added, "I'm afraid your presence might distract Dr. Grimes too much. Better run along."

"All right. Shall I tell Mom you'll both be home for dinner?"

"It may be rather late," Professor Bullfinch answered. "You may as well tell her," he added, with a glance at the government agent, "that there will be three of us."

The children left the barn.

Irene said, "It's not even noon. It feels as though we've been away in a foreign land for years and years."

They went round to the end of the building and tried to find the crack through which they had emerged at the start of their adventure.

"I think that's it," Danny said, indicating a place where the boards gaped. "It's awfully hard to tell from this height."

"I think you may be right," said Irene. "Look, there's the tin can we passed. And surely that's the patch of clover where we had some nectar?"

"It's so tiny," Danny said. "I wonder if that's my butterfly?"

Joe had been muttering to himself. Now he said, "Stand back."

They moved away, startled.

"What's the trouble?" Dan asked.

"Nothing. I have just finished a poem," said Joe. "And you are the first to hear it. Aren't you lucky?"

"I'll tell you later," Danny said.

Joe ignored him, and began to recite:

> "If I could be the size of a mouse
> With an ice-cream soda as high as a house
>   I'd be gay.
> Or if I could be as tall as a tree
> With my school-teacher only as high as my knee
>   I would stay
>   That way.
> If I were big and my homework small
> I wouldn't mind that
>   At all, at all.
> Or I could be short with a long vacation
>   What a sensation!
> Any size is okay by me
> If the good things are large and
>   the bad ones wee.
> You see?"

"I agree," said Danny, promptly.

"So do—er—me," said Irene.

Joe snorted. "Oh, great! Everybody wants to be a poet," he said. "Come on, Cecil. Let's go find it."

His friends ran after him, laughing.

"Find what?" Irene said, as they linked arms with him.

"An ice-cream soda that's just the right size for lunch," said Joe.

And off they went.

Jay Williams, co-author of the Danny Dunn books, has been a professional writer for the past twenty-seven years. To his credit are twenty-five fiction and non-fiction titles for children of all ages, *in addition to* the eleven books about Danny. Parents, teachers, librarians, reviewers, and especially little children have found THE COOKIE TREE, THE QUESTION BOX, PHILBERT THE FEARFUL, and THE PRACTICAL PRINCESS memorable and enchanting tales. Mr. Williams also has an enviable reputation on both sides of the Atlantic as an author of adult novels of which UNIAD (Scribner's) is the most recent. Born in Buffalo, New York, he was educated at the University of Pennsylvania, Columbia University, and the Art Students' League. Now, Mr. Williams and his family live in England—where, perhaps at this very moment, he is reading a letter from a young fan who has written to suggest the plot of the next suspense-filled scientific adventure for their hero, Danny Dunn.

Raymond Abrashkin authored and co-produced the very popular and successful "Little Fugitive" which won an award at the Venice Film Festival.

About the Artist

Paul Sagsoorian was born in New York. He studied art at several art schools in New York City, and also went to the Map Making School of the U. S. Army. In 1957, the American Institute of Graphic Arts selected a book illustrated by Paul Sagsoorian as one of the Fifty Best Books of the year. Mr. Sagsoorian has been free-lancing since he completed his art training. Now, he works for art studios, advertising agencies, and book publishers.